A Note to Parents

DK READERS is a compelling program  designed in conjunction with leading lit Dr. Linda Gambrell, Professor of Educa University. Dr. Gambrell has served as Reading Conference and the College Reading Association, and has recently been elected to serve as President of the International Reading Association.

Beautiful illustrations and superb full-color photographs combine with engaging, easy-to-read stories and informational texts to offer a fresh approach to each subject in the series. Each DK READER is guaranteed to capture a child's interest while developing his or her reading skills, general knowledge, and love of reading.

The five levels of DK READERS are aimed at different reading abilities, enabling you to choose the books that are exactly right for your child:

> **Pre-level 1**: Learning to read
>
> **Level 1**: Beginning to read
>
> **Level 2**: Beginning to read alone
>
> **Level 3**: Reading alone
>
> **Level 4**: Proficient readers

The "normal" age at which a child begins to read can be anywhere from three to eight years old. Adult participation through the lower levels is very helpful for providing encouragement, discussing storylines, and sounding out unfamiliar words.

No matter which level you select, you can be sure that you are helping your child learn to read, then read to learn!

LONDON, NEW YORK, MUNICH,
MELBOURNE, AND DELHI

Project Editor Amy Junor
Designer Thelma-Jane Robb
Brand Manager Lisa Lanzarini
Publishing Manager Simon Beecroft
Category Publisher Alex Allan
Print Production Nick Seston
Production Editor Siu Chan

Reading Consultant
Linda Gambrell

First published in the United States in 2008 by
DK Publishing , 375 Hudson Street,
New York, New York 10014

08 09 10 11 10 9 8 7 6 5 4 3 2

PD238 – 02/08

DK Books are available at special discounts when
purchased in bulk for sales promotions, premiums,
fund-raising, or educational use.
For details, contact: DK Publishing Special Markets,
375 Hudson Street,
New York, New York 10014
SpecialSales@dk.com

A catalog record for this book is available
from the Library of Congress.

ISBN: 978-0-7566-3492-6 (paperback)
ISBN: 978-0-7566-3493-3 (hardback)

Color reproduction by GRB Editrice S.r.l., London
Printed and bound by Lake Book Manufacturing, Inc., U.S.A.

Written by Simon Beecroft

POWER RANGERS S.P.D.

Space Patrol Delta is a group of specially trained Power Rangers.

Space Patrol Delta is also known as S.P.D. Its mission is to guard Earth from danger!

In the year 2025,
many aliens from outer space live
peacefully with humans.
But some aliens are dangerous.
They want to start a war with Earth!

S.P.D.'s A-Squad was Earth's first line of defence. But then A-Squad disappeared without trace. So a replacement squad had to step in—the B-Squad Rangers.

Blue Ranger, Red Ranger, and Green Ranger are members of B-Squad. Sometimes they argue with each other. But they always help each other in battle.

Blue Ranger wanted to be the leader, but he was chosen to be second in command. He flies a special flying vehicle. Blue Ranger can also make force fields. These invisible shields protect him from attacks.

Red Ranger is the leader of B-Squad.

Red Ranger drives a patrol bike and has the power to pass through solid objects.

Green Ranger's special power is the ability to read people's minds.

Zords
Power Rangers use robotic vehicles called zords to help them defeat monsters.

Sometimes the Power Rangers face an enemy that is too big or powerful for them to defeat individually. Then, their zord vehicles connect together to form a much more powerful robot called a megazord.

S.P.D. B-Squad's megazord is made up of six individual zords.

Megazord
Megazords have special powers and weapons which make them strong in battle.

Mystic Force is a group of
five Power Rangers with magic
powers and incredible
martial arts skills.

The Mystic Force Power
Rangers must save Earth from an
evil warrior called the Master of
the Underworld. The Master
appears as a flaming skull
carried by tentacles. He leads
an army of terrifying monsters.

The Master wants to rule the
human and the magical world.

Each Mystic Force Power Rangers has a magic power. The Red Mystic Ranger is the leader. He has power over fire.

The Green Mystic Ranger gets his power from the Earth.

The Yellow Mystic Ranger has the ability to use the power of lightning. He carries a crossbow that fires bolts of electricity.

Crossbow
A crossbow is a special kind of bow and arrow. The bow is fixed to a wooden pole.

The Pink and Blue Mystic Rangers are sisters.

The Pink Mystic Ranger is tough and strong. She always looks out for her friends and her sister. She can command the power of the wind. In battle, she can turn herself into a fierce tornado.

The Blue Mystic Ranger is calmer than her sister. Her power is water. In battle, she can release water blasts at her opponents.

Tornado
A tornado is a powerful, twisting wind storm.

The Mystic Force Power Rangers roar into battle on their Mystic Racers. These powerful flying vehicles can travel at high speeds. They can also launch rockets and fire laser blasts.

Laser blast
A laser blast is an explosive missile made of powerful lightbeams.

When the Mystic Racers are not in use, they turn into wooden brooms. The brooms hang on the wall in the Mystic Rangers' command center.

Even with their magic powers, the Mystic Force Power Rangers cannot defeat the evil Master of the Underworld. They must transform into super-powerful Mystic Titans!

Green Ranger is the largest Mystic Titan. He has bull's horns and uses an ax in battle.

As a Mystic Titan, Yellow Ranger has wings instead of arms.

Red Ranger becomes a Mystic Ranger knight. He carries a giant sword.

The Mystic Force Power
Rangers have one more magical
ability to use against the Master
of the Underworld's army.

They can join together in
Mystic Titan forms to
create a Mystic Dragon.

Red Ranger
in his Mystic
Titan form
rides the giant
Mystic Dragon.

Now the Power Rangers cannot
fail to defeat the forces of evil!

Dragon
In myths and legends, a dragon is a flying lizard that can breathe fire.

The Operation Overdrive Power Rangers are five brave, skilled, and adventurous teenagers.

Their mission is to search for some magical jewels that were stolen long ago and hidden around the world.

The leader of the Operation Overdrive Power Rangers is the Red Ranger. He has superhuman strength. His weapon is a special spear.

Dump Driver
Red Ranger drives a zord called a Dump Driver. It is equipped with lasers and claws.

The Black Ranger
is a spy-for-hire.
His special powers are
superhuman hearing
and sight.

Sometimes the
Black Ranger
wields a giant
hammer called
the Drive
Slammer.
He can throw
the Drive
Slammer and
it returns like
a boomerang.

When the Black Ranger strikes the Drive Slammer against the ground, it can create deep holes.

Speed Driver
The Black Ranger's zord is a racing car called the Speed Driver. It can reach high speeds and is equipped with missiles.

The Blue Ranger worked in Hollywood as a stunt man. He was also a bit of a practical joker. His special power is the ability to leap great distances.

One of the Blue Ranger's weapons is a handheld fan called the Drive Vortex. It can create strong winds.

Gyro Driver
The Blue Ranger's zord is a special plane called the Gyro Driver.

The Blue Ranger can also use the Drive Vortex to propel himself into the air or launch a whirlwind blast.

The Power Rangers must stop two dangerous criminals from finding the magical jewels. The jewels would give the criminals ultimate power.

The Power Rangers join together all their zords into one giant Megazord. Now the Power Rangers are unbeatable!

Power vehicles
The Yellow Ranger's zord is a bulldozer and the Pink Ranger's zord is a submarine.

1 What does S.P.D. stand for?

2 Power Rangers use special robotic vehicles to help them defeat villains. What are these vehicles called?

3 Mystic Force Power Rangers fight an evil warrior. What is he called?

4 The Pink and Blue Mystic Force Power Rangers are related. How are they related?

5 What are the Mystic Force Power Rangers' super-powerful forms called?

6 In their super-powerful forms, what can the Mystic Force Power Rangers combine together to form?

7 The Operation Overdrive Power Rangers are looking for precious, magical objects. What are they?

8 Who is the leader of the Operation Overdrive Power Rangers?

9 Operation Overdrive's Blue Ranger worked in Hollywood. What work did he do?

10 Name one of the special vehicles used by the Operation Overdrive Power Rangers.

Answers

1 Space Patrol Delta
2 Zords
3 The Master of the Underworld
4 They are sisters
5 Mystic Titans
6 A Mystic Dragon

7 Jewels
8 Red Ranger
9 He was a stunt man
10 Dump Driver, Speed Driver, Gyro Driver, bulldozer, or submarine